DISNEY
Phineas and Ferb

CANDACE
AGAINST THE UNIVERSE

Adapted by Steve Behling

Based on the series created by
Dan Povenmire & Jeff "Swampy" Marsh

DISNEY PRESS
Los Angeles • New York

First Paperback Edition, November 2020 10 9 8 7 6 5 4 3 2 1

ISBN 978-1-368-06197-1
FAC-025438-20283
Library of Congress Control Number: 2020940247
Printed in the United States of America
Visit www.disneybooks.com

SUSTAINABLE
FORESTRY
INITIATIVE

Certified Sourcing

www.sfiprogram.org
SFI-01054
The SFI label applies to the text stock

Chapter 1

"MOOOOOOOOOOOMMMMM!"
Candace Flynn screamed into her cell phone.
On the other end was her mom.

"Okay, Candace, " Mom said.
"What is it this time?"

"It's . . . it's . . . it's hard to
explain!" Candace said.

Candace was looking at her
backyard, where her brothers,
Phineas and Ferb, were being juggled by a giant
robot, along with their friends Buford and Baljeet,
along with Isabella and her Fireside Girls troop.
Candace couldn't stand that her brothers were
once again doing whatever they wanted and

having a great time and not getting busted.

That was what she was doing: busting them.

"Where are you?" Candace asked frantically.

"I'm almost home," Mom said.

That made Candace very happy. At last Mom would see exactly what Phineas and Ferb were up to, and they'd get busted!

* * *

Hey! Where's Perry?

* * *

Meanwhile, Perry the Platypus was confronting his archnemesis, Doctor Heinz Doofenshmirtz.

They were fighting on the balcony of Doofenshmirtz Evil, Incorporated, Doofenshmirtz's headquarters.

"It's too late, Perry the Platypus!" the doctor said. "My Power-Vacuum-inator will soon turn the mayor's mansion into lint and then vacuum it up, thereby creating an actual 'power vacuum'

2

for me to fill! See? See how I used 'vacuum' as both a transitive verb *and* an abstract concept? That's grammatical versatility!"

Perry grabbed a vacuum cleaner and hurled it at the devious doctor. Doof smacked right into the Power-Vacuum-inator, activating the device. A beam of purple light erupted from the machine. . . .

* * *

The purple ray zipped across the sky of Danville and just happened to hit the giant robot in Phineas and Ferb's backyard. The robot turned into a giant vaguely robot-shaped piece of lint just as Mom's car pulled into the driveway.

"It's . . . I don't know what it is, but it's still here!" Candace said.

* * *

3

"I see what you did there," Dr. Doofenshmirtz said as the Power-Vacuum-inator started to suck in air. "You used 'vacuum' as a noun *and* as a weapon. Touché."

* * *

Candace tried to get her mom to see what Phineas and Ferb were up to. But Mom wasn't having it. "Every day you call and tell me Phineas and Ferb have built some big, unbelievable thing in the backyard, and every day I come home to find nothing there. Doesn't it exhaust you?"

"I am begging you! I—I—" Candace sputtered.

"It exhausts me," Mom said. At last, she looked in the backyard. "Oh, look! There's nothing here."

Mom carried some groceries inside, leaving Candace alone as the friends departed.

"It's not fair," Candace said, fuming.

"Did you say something, Candace?" Phineas asked.

"I said, it's not *fair*," she repeated. "Every day always works out for you. You guys are having a great summer!"

"Well, we're all having a pretty great—" Phineas started.

"*Not me*, okay?!" Candace shouted. "Every day, I get beaten down by the universe. I just feel so defeated. I feel so alone!"

Candace began to sob as she walked away from her brothers. Neither knew exactly what to do or how to comfort her.

"Wow," Phineas said. "We've been having so much fun this summer I just assumed Candace had been, too. We should do something to cheer her up. We should make her a gift! Let's see. Last time, we carved her face into Mount Rushmore. Let's do something more permanent this time!"

So the boys went inside the house to think of the ultimate gift for their sister.

5

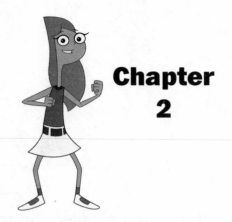

Chapter 2

Candace sat on the front steps, crying her eyes out, thinking about the universe and how it was against her. She wasn't sure exactly how much it was against her. The sound of a moped interrupted Candace's reverie, and she looked up to see a young woman riding the vehicle. The woman took off her helmet, revealing long black hair underneath.

"Candace?" the woman said.

"Oh, hey, Vanessa," Candace said, still crying.

"I thought that was you. Is this your house?" Vanessa asked. She was wearing all black, as befitted the daughter of Dr. Heinz Doofenshmirtz.

"Yep," Candace replied. "My house of pain.

My brothers get away with some big, ridiculous thing, and yet somehow, *I'm* the crazy one! It's like the whole universe is against me!"

Vanessa gently suggested that maybe, possibly, that wasn't really the universe's fault and also that maybe, possibly, the universe wasn't against Candace.

"You're right!" Candace said. "It's mostly Phineas and Ferb's fault! That's why I have to bust them!"

Vanessa raised an eyebrow. "Have you ever considered *not* trying to bust your brothers? I mean, let's say you *did* finally expose them. Then what? Would you suddenly be happy? Would all your problems just magically disappear?"

"*Yes!*" Candace shouted.

"Maybe. Maybe not," Vanessa continued. "Is it possible that your obsession with busting them is really just a distraction from your real problem— which is how you feel about yourself?"

Candace stared at Vanessa, thinking. "You mean like a tiny, meaningless speck in the universe, completely overshadowed by Phineas and Ferb?"

"That's good," Vanessa said. "Keep going. . . ."

"Everybody thinks my brothers are so special!" Candace said. "Well, what about *me*? When do I get to feel special?"

"Yes?" Vanessa said, trying to be encouraging.

Candace frowned. "And . . . what if I'm not?"

Vanessa leaned close to Candace and put a comforting hand on her shoulder.

"I can't believe this," Candace said.

"I know, it's kind of a breakthrough, right?" Vanessa said. "But now the healing can beg—"

"I can't believe *this*!" Candace shouted. She pointed to a strange futuristic pod that was sitting on her front lawn! Candace moved right past Vanessa to check out the weird contraption.

"See?" Candace said. "*This* is the kind of insane stuff I'm talking about. Okay, guys, I give up, what does this one do? Phineas and Ferb, I know you're in there!"

Candace banged a

fist against the metal pod. Suddenly, panels on the roof opened, and something resembling a giant funnel emerged.

"Um . . . if you don't know what it does, maybe you shouldn't hit it?" Vanessa suggested.

"Relax. It's probably some kind of amusement park ride or it makes giant waffles or something," Candace said nonchalantly.

Before Candace could hit the machine again, the big funnel above them began sucking up grass and dirt from the yard. A second later, the funnel  sucked up Candace and Vanessa.

In a flash, Candace and Vanessa found  themselves landing on a cold metal floor. They were inside the pod! They rushed to the windows. They could see Candace's house outside.

The pod began to vibrate, and the sound of rockets igniting filled the room.

Then Candace saw Phineas and Ferb leave the house. Phineas looked like he was holding a present.

"Phineas! Ferb!" Candace cried out.

But it was too late.

* * *

"Candace! Where are you going?" Phineas shouted as he looked at his sister in the window of the pod. "Where is she going?"

Ferb didn't say a word. He just snapped a picture of the pod as it flew away.

Chapter 3

Meanwhile, Perry the Platypus had returned to the Flynn-Fletcher household and was sleeping under a tree. He was no longer in secret agent mode. No, he was now just an average platypus, a pet so common that you see them almost as often as you see cats or dogs.

Perry's nap was interrupted by an alert from his wrist communicator. A secret door in the tree behind him opened, and Perry rolled through it. He slid down a long

tube until he found himself inside his secret lair. As he landed in his chair, a video screen before him hummed to life. A gray-haired man with a mustache and a smart-looking uniform appeared.

"Agent P, we've just received automated emergency alert 136 Alpha," Major Monogram said. Major Monogram was Perry's superior at the OWCA, an organization devoted to fighting evil. "We have . . . no idea what that is, but Carl is looking it up in the owner's manual."

Carl, an intern, popped up behind Major Monogram and handed him a book.

"Apparently," Major Monogram said, reading from the book, "it is a . . . 'clogged intake valve'?" Major Monogram looked more closely at the book. "Carl, this is for the washing machine."

"Wait, hold on," Carl said, digging through more manuals. "This is for the stereo. . . . Microwave instructions . . . Oh! Here it is!"

Carl handed the real manual to Monogram. "Now let's see here. . . . 'A member of your host family has been abducted by aliens.'"

Behind Monogram, a photograph of Candace appeared. "This is priority one, Agent P. But remember, you cannot reveal to her that you are a secret agent, so . . . guess it's gonna be tricky

to rescue her. Heh. Well, good luck with that."

Perry rolled his eyes, then saluted Major Monogram. Then he pressed a button and blasted out of his lair on his chair. (Hey, that rhymed!)

* * *

Phineas and Ferb were in their bedroom, analyzing the photo Ferb had taken just minutes before. They zoomed in on various parts of the alien pod, looking for clues. Clicking on the window, they saw Candace inside, screaming.

"You're right, Ferb," Phineas said. "It doesn't look like she did this on purpose. What's that little rectangle down there?"

Ferb zoomed in on the side of the pod.

"Bingo!" Phineas said. "Alien license plate.

She's been abducted by aliens! Let's run those tags on the Galactic Web."

Without missing a beat, Ferb's fingers danced along the computer keyboard and brought up the Galactic Web search page. Typing in the numbers, Ferb immediately got a hit. "It's from planet Feebla-Oot in the Vroblok Cluster," he said.

"That must be where they're taking her. Ferb, I know what we're gonna do today! We're going to an alien planet to rescue our sister!" Phineas announced.

They stared at each other for a moment, both realizing something important.

"I guess first we have to figure out how to get to the, uh, Vrobl—the Vro—"

"The Vroblok Cluster," Ferb said.

"The Vroblok Cluster," Phineas said. "Man, try saying that five times fast."

Then Ferb said "Vroblok" five times fast, immediately followed by Phineas doing so, thus proving that it was, in fact, *not* hard to say "Vroblok" five times fast.

14

Chapter 4

Candace and Vanessa sat on the cold metal floor of the pod. Vanessa was throwing a ball against the wall opposite her, playing catch by herself.

"Okay," Candace finally said. "This is *not* one of Phineas and Ferb's inventions."

"How can you tell?" Vanessa asked.

"'Cause of *that*!" Candace said, pointing at the window.

Vanessa looked out the window,

and they saw that their pod was approaching an enormous alien mother ship. Other pods similar to the one that had captured them approached the mother ship from all directions and docked.

"Looks like we're not the only ones being brought here," Vanessa observed.

"What do you think they want from us?" Candace wondered.

"Best-case scenario?" Vanessa said. "We're food."

"That's your best-case scenario?" Candace  said, amazed. "Man, you are dark."

* * *

Back on Earth, Phineas and Ferb had just rung the doorbell at their friend Baljeet's house. Baljeet answered the door, decked out in fan gear celebrating one of his favorite television shows, *Space Adventure*.

"Oh, hey, guys!" Baljeet said cheerfully. "You came at a great time! I was just about to start watching my box set of *Space Adventure*!"

"Actually," Phineas said, "Candace got abducted by aliens and taken to another planet. And we need your help to rescue her."

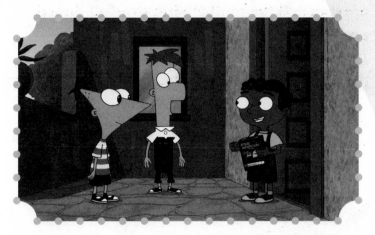

"Well, why did you not lead with that?" Baljeet replied. "I suppose you will want me to build another portal. Where is the planet?"

Ferb offered him a piece of paper with the coordinates of planet Feebla-Oot. Baljeet took the paper and eyed the numbers carefully.

"That is like eight systems away," Baljeet said. "We will need a much more powerful quantum field generator."

"But could we do it?" Phineas asked hopefully.

"Yes, but even if we got the whole gang together, it would still take at least a whole chapter of us constructing it."

Chapter 5

"Aaaand we're done!" Buford said as he and Isabella put the finishing touches on the Transportation Portal.

"Well, I guess it only took a page turn," Baljeet said.

"So this portal will take us to the same planet they're taking Candace to?" Isabella asked.

Phineas nodded. "Yep, when we step through this portal, we're going to be on an alien planet, and we have no idea what to expect."

"Actually, I took the liberty of printing out some possible scenarios based on the infinite possibilities," Baljeet said. "We could be attacked by carnivorous plants, giant alien spiders, flying shark creatures. . . ."

"Are any *not* terrifying?" Isabella inquired.

"Oh, of course!" Baljeet said. "Here is a bunch of playful puppies—"

"Awwwww!" Isabella swooned.

"—that shoot nerve gas from their tongues."

"Ewwwww," Isabella said.

Phineas stared at his friends. "Look, what Baljeet is saying is this could get really dangerous. Ferb and I can't ask you to go. Candace is *our* sister. She was pretty upset the last time we saw her. And I kinda feel like somehow it's our fault," he said. "So we're the ones who have to make this right. This isn't on you."

"If you think you're goin' to an alien planet without us, you're even crazier than Candace," Buford said.

"Yeah! Bring on the nerve gas puppies!" Isabella said enthusiastically.

"Thank you, guys," Phineas said, touched. "Ready? Here we go!"

The group joined hands and stepped through the portal. . . .

* * *

"Hello! And welcome, aliens!"

As the kids emerged from the other side of the portal, they were greeted by a large robot.

Baljeet screamed.

"Oh, that's just Norm," Dr. Doofenshmirtz said. "He's usually harmless. Um, are you aliens?"

"*You're* the alien!" Buford said.

Isabella looked over the balcony. "Guys, we're still in Danville!"

And they were! At Doofenshmirtz Evil, Incorporated, to be precise.

"This is not possible," Baljeet said. "My calculations could not have been *that* off."

Phineas saw that Dr. Doofenshmirtz had a similar-looking portal. "And why do you have a portal?" he asked.

"Well, I was trying to get to the planet Feebla-Oot," the doctor replied.

"We have to get to Feebla-Oot to save our sister!" Phineas told him.

"My daughter was apparently abducted by an alien pod from there!" Dr. Doofenshmirtz added. "She posted about it on the social media."

The doctor held up his cell phone, showing a

picture of his daughter, Vanessa, in the alien pod. Candace was with her.

"Wait, that's Vanessa," Phineas said. "We know her!"

"And she's with Candace!" Isabella interjected.

"Oh, I hope my little girl is okay," Dr. Doofenshmirtz said, worried.

"Wha-haaaa!" Baljeet said, staring at his phone. "There is an ion barrier around the planet. Our transporters were both deflected, which made them connect to each other!"

There was silence for a moment as the group looked at each other, wondering what they could possibly do. At last, Phineas spoke. "If we're going to rescue Candace and Vanessa, we need to build a spaceship," he said. Looking around Dr. Doofenshmirtz's place, Phineas saw all kinds of machines. "Unless anyone has one lying around."

"I don't have a spaceship per se," Dr. Doofenshmirtz said, "but I *do* have . . ."

The kids were in suspense as Dr. Doofenshmirtz unveiled what looked exactly like a spaceship on the balcony.

". . . my Galactic-Travel-inator!" the doctor announced proudly. "You get inside it and it flies you up to and through space."

"You mean like a spaceship?" Isabella said.

"Well, I suppose it is *like* a spaceship in that it *operates* exactly like, and performs the same *functions* as, a spaceship, but it's an -inator," Dr. Doofenshmirtz explained. "There's a difference."

Everyone agreed that it didn't matter what it was called as long as it could take them to Candace and Vanessa. So the group began loading supplies onto the spaceship-that-wasn't-a-spaceship.

No one saw the portal fire up one more time, and no one observed the platypus wearing a fedora emerge. . . .

Chapter 6

The kids were still loading supplies onto Dr. Doofenshmirtz's spaceship-that-wasn't-a-spaceship when Isabella noticed a particularly weird-looking device and said, "Is that something we're gonna need?"

"Let's just say that I'd rather have a device that  makes things switch places with the nearest chicken and not need it than need one and not have it," the doctor explained.

"I'm with him on that," Buford agreed as he carried a canoe aboard the ship-or-whatever-it-was.

"Says the guy bringing a canoe into space," Isabella replied.

* * *

Hiding behind an -inator, Agent P used his secret wrist communicator to communicate with Major Monogram. Secretly.

"Remember, you can't reveal yourself as an agent to your host family, but you also can't reveal yourself as their pet to Dr. Doofenshmirtz. I guess in retrospect, you are the single worst agent we could've sent  on this mission," Major Monogram said.

The screen cut out, and Agent P rolled his eyes. Then he scrambled past an -inator and boarded the ship unseen.

* * *

"Is there a barf bag on this thing, Doc?" Buford said. "I'm asking for a friend."

"All right, Operation: Save Candace and Vanessa is about to begin!" Phineas announced.

The kids had boarded the it's-obviously-a-spaceship with Dr. Doofenshmirtz, along with all their supplies, like the canoe and the thing that replaced chickens. Isabella looked at Phineas and pressed the ignition button. The ship (it's definitely a ship) shook and rumbled as it began to lift off from the balcony. Flames from the rocket engines seared the building, setting it on fire.

"Oh, no!" Dr. Doofenshmirtz said, looking out the window at the fire. "Okay, that was poor planning. That was on me. But so fun to be traveling into outer space with a bunch of kids who teleported into my house with no adult supervision. What are all your names again?"

Chapter 7

Candace and Vanessa emerged from their pod, cautiously walking down the hallway of the alien mother ship. They passed pod after pod, looking inside.

"Empty . . . empty . . . empty," Candace said quietly. "Are we the only ones they abducted?"

Before Vanessa could answer, they heard footsteps coming their way on the metallic floor. The girls ducked into an alcove just in time to avoid being seen by a shadowy figure. The footsteps faded away, and Candace let out a sigh of relief. She tilted her head as she spotted something on the wall she hadn't seen before. It looked like a touch screen map of the mother ship.

."I wish we could read these weird markings," Candace said.

A computer voice said, "English detected. Would you like me to change the map settings to English?"

"Oh, yes!" Candace said enthusiastically.

At once, the text on the map reconfigured itself until it was all in English.

"Computer, how do we escape from this ship?" Candace asked.

"Adding 'thin chips' to your shopping list," the computer responded.

"No, no, no, no. I said 'escape the ship,'" Candace repeated.

"Playing 'Cape Lip' by Lil' Gorbinox," the computer replied.

Music started to play, and Candace shrugged.

She read aloud from the map. "Engine room . . . sick bay . . . Ooh! Smoothie bar!"

"Focus," Vanessa urged her.

"Sorry," Candace said.

Then she saw a section that said ESCAPE PODS.

Candace pressed a button on the wall, and an elevator opened. At least, she thought it was an elevator. There was no elevator car inside. It was just a long shaft with a ladder on the side.

With no other choice but to climb down, Vanessa entered the shaft, followed by Candace.

"You know, I'm still blaming Phineas and Ferb for this," Candace said.

"How so, exactly?" Vanessa asked.

"Well, if I hadn't been thinking about how they ruined my life, I might have seen that this came from outer space and therefore was *not* one of their inventions."

"Yeah, that makes complete sense," Vanessa said, meaning exactly the opposite.

At last, they reached the bottom of the mother ship. The girls were surrounded by twenty or so escape pods that ringed the circular wall. Vanessa remained at the door to make sure no one was coming while Candace checked out the room.

"Okay, I found the escape pods," she said.

"Opening escape pods," the computer replied.

With a *whoosh*, an escape pod opened.

There was another noise: footsteps, this time above them. Vanessa turned her head and saw shadows moving in an opening above.

Aliens!

"We've got to go now!" Vanessa said, hitting a

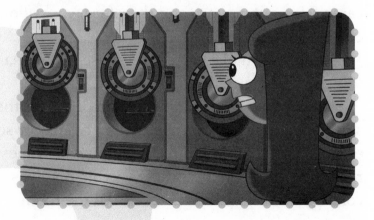

button on the touch screen. She jumped into an escape pod.

"Wait, there's only room for—" Vanessa started.

"You take this one," Candace said. They could hear the aliens descending the ladder tube. "I'll be right behind you. See you back on Earth!" Then she leaned into the control panel. "Computer, launch the escape pod."

"Launching all escape pods," the computer said.

Suddenly, the hatches on *all* the escape pods closed and they ejected into space!

Chapter 8

"According to my calculations, we are on course to reach the planet in forty-seven minutes at our current velocity," Baljeet said.

Baljeet and Ferb were busy reading a star chart, trying to get their navigational bearings. Isabella and Dr. Doofenshmirtz were sitting in the pilot and copilot seats while Phineas stood behind them.

Buford was doing tricks with his yo-yo.

A light on the dashboard began to flash, and then came a *THWOCK!* sound as something hit the ship's hull.

"What was *that*?" Phineas asked.

"Oh, no!" Baljeet said. "We are entering an uncharted asteroid field!"

Everyone strapped in as Isabella and Dr.
Doofenshmirtz grabbed the controls.

* * *

Behind them, unnoticed by everyone, Agent P
hid behind the bulkhead. He moved quickly into
the ship's air lock and put on a pressure suit. Then
he entered the cold void of space.

Attached to the ship via tether, Agent P used his
trusty jet pack to maneuver toward a humongous
asteroid that was on a collision course with the ship.

Firing his grappling hook, Agent P hit the huge asteroid. Then, using his momentum, he managed to swing it toward another asteroid.

THWOCK!
THWOCK!

But yet another asteroid was coming right for him! Thinking fast, Agent P deployed his emergency parachute. Using it like a gigantic

sling, he caught the asteroid and deflected it from the ship.

"Wow, it's like the Fourth of July out there," Dr. Doofenshmirtz observed.

"Somehow we're missing all the asteroids," Isabella said, noticing the curious fact that a lot of the huge rocks seemed to be avoiding them. But how was that possible?

"Hey, everybody—look!" Buford shouted.

Everyone shifted their attention toward Buford, who was holding his yo-yo, swinging it back and forth in a configuration of string. "Cat's cradle!" he said proudly. "It's the first time I've ever been able to do this!"

"Hey, we're out of the asteroid field!" Dr. Doofenshmirtz said brightly.

Agent P clung to the back of the ship, asteroids now safely behind them. He scampered to the air lock, went inside the ship, and closed the hatch.

35

Chapter 9

"Uh-oh," Vanessa said, looking through the small window on her escape pod. "That does *not* look like Earth."

The reason it didn't look like Earth was that it was not. It was the planet Feebla-Oot.

Vanessa braced herself as the escape pod entered the planet's atmosphere. At last it came to a stop on the ground, and the hatch opened.

Dusting herself off, Vanessa exited the pod.

"I guess Candace should be coming right behind me," she said hopefully.

As if on cue, a fleet of escape pods thundered down from the sky. They were heading right for her. Vanessa screamed and sprinted as fast as she could. The last

one landed only inches away from her.

"Candace?" Vanessa asked as the escape pod popped open.

But there was no one inside.

A loud rumble caught her attention, and Vanessa's eyes drifted skyward. She saw the mother ship as it entered Feebla-Oot's atmosphere and set down on a landing pad connected to a fortress in the distance.

"What good are escape pods if they take you *to* the planet you're trying to escape *from*?" Vanessa wondered aloud.

* * *

Candace was marched down the ramp of the mother ship by the aliens.

"Where are you taking me?" she asked.

They stopped in front of a large door. A voice called from inside. "Just come on in!"

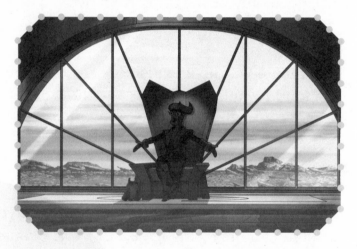

The aliens escorted Candace into a room where a large, impressive-looking alien sat.

"Come here," said the alien. "Let me get a look at you. You are spectacular. Where are my manners? I'm Super Super Big Doctor."

"Is that . . . is that a title?" Candace asked. "Or your . . ."

"It's a common enough name in our language," Super Super Big Doctor said defensively. "I mean, it's not Eegblat or Boat Jelly, but it's a name you hear."

"Oh . . . uh, nice to meet you," Candace said. "My name's Candace."

At the mention of her name, a collective gasp filled the room.

"What did I say?" Candace asked, confused.

"Ooh, sorry," Super Super Big Doctor said. "In our language, 'candace' is the noise someone makes when they explode from the waist up."

"I'm sorry, does that happen often enough that you—" Candace started.

"What matters is we found you," Super Super Big Doctor said, cutting her off. "And you are the Chosen One!

"We have spent *years* searching the galaxy for Remarkalonium, a rare element we desperately

need. And our instruments tell us that that element simply emanates from you. You, Candy Cane—can I call you Candy Cane?—just by existing, you are saving our planet."

Candace blushed. "Okay, this is amazing! And just to be clear—this 'saving the world' thing doesn't involve offering me as a human sacrifice?"

Super Super Big Doctor chuckled. "Well, *some*body's paranoid."

"Sorry, it's—it's just . . . I've always felt the universe was against me. I have these annoying little brothers who always get away with everything," Candace said.

"Shut . . . *up!*" Super Super Big Doctor exclaimed. "I grew up with annoying little brothers, too! Always messing around, getting away with everything. But I'm supposed to be in charge!"

"*Yes!*" Candace cried. "Exactly! And not just conditionally!"

"That's why I came to this planet," Super

Super Big Doctor said. "And now I really *am* in charge. It's perfection."

"Wow," Candace said, her eyes widening. "Maybe the universe *isn't* against me."

"Welcome to Feebla-Oot," Super Super Big Doctor said. "All hail the Chosen One!"

"All hail the Chosen One!" shouted the assembled crowd of aliens.

Chapter 10

"Okay, we are approaching the ion barrier," Baljeet said. "Activate your ion shield."

Dr. Doofenshmirtz looked at the controls. "We don't have an ion shield," he said. "We're not fancy-shmancy."

"But we have to pass through an ion barrier to get to the planet," Baljeet insisted. "If we go through the ion barrier without a shield, it could fry all of the electronics on the ship, rendering our navigation useless and stranding us in space."

"Well, there's got to be a way through, right?" Phineas said.

"No . . ." Baljeet said, his voice trailing off. "Wait a minute! In Episode 206B

of *Space Adventure*, they were able to go through an ion barrier without a shield by spinning the USS *Minotaur* and scattering the ions as they went!"

Isabella raised an eyebrow. "I'm not sure that would work in real life. . . ."

"Well, I am sure that the writers of *Space Adventure* have a better grasp of astrophysics than you . . . or even me, because I do not see how the science would work, either," Baljeet said. "Buuuut . . . Hold on!"

Without warning, Baljeet grabbed the controls, forcing the ship into a spin, just like the USS

Minotaur in episode whatever of *Space Adventure*.

And apparently, the episode was right, and so was the science, because it worked! The ship made it through the ion barrier, and nothing terrible happened!

Except the ship couldn't . . . stop . . . *spinning*!

"We're clear, Baljeet!" Phineas said. "You can stop it spinning now!"

"Unfortunately, I cannot!" Baljeet exclaimed. "We have lost all helm control!"

"What?!" said Buford, who was surprisingly not doing any yo-yo tricks.

"I do not understand," Baljeet said. "It worked perfectly in *Space Adventure*!"

The ship continued to spin as it brushed up against the atmosphere of the nearest planet.

Inside, the kids and Dr. Doofenshmirtz (and

presumably Agent P, who was still hiding) were tossed about the cabin.

Phineas managed to get a look at one of the monitors and said, "Well, there is some good news! That planet we're plummeting towards is Feebla-Oot . . . so we're crashing right on target! We're coming, Candace!"

* * *

One crash later, the kids and Dr. Doofenshmirtz found themselves on the strange alien landscape of Feebla-Oot.

"Look at all the damage!" Isabella said, walking around the ship. "We're not getting anywhere in this spaceship."

"I am not sure how we will ever get back home," Baljeet said sadly.

Fortunately—and remarkably—Buford's canoe was still intact.

"We'll figure out something," Phineas said, trying to raise everyone's spirits. "We always do! But the important thing is we have to find Candace and Vanessa. They're counting on us!"

"Maybe we should start by looking there," Isabella said, pointing toward an imposing fortress ahead.

"Good eye," Phineas said. "I hate to think what
Candace is going through in there. This must
be the worst day of her life."

Chapter 11

"This is the best day of my life!"

Candace sat in a lounge chair right next to Super Super Big Doctor, eating tiny appetizers as aliens massaged her feet.

"Stapler Fist there is my toughest guard,"

Super Super Big Doctor said. "But boy, if he doesn't give the finest foot massages."

Stapler Fist massaged Candace's feet, then gave her an icy stare, awaiting her verdict.

"The pressure is perfect, Mr. Fist."

Suddenly, Stapler Fist's entire demeanor changed, and he became overjoyed. "OMG! The Chosen One spoke to me!" he said. "I can't believe it. I'm so excited I could actually explode. Seriously, I could just—"

Suddenly, there was a sound like someone with a really low voice saying *"Candace!"* and Stapler Fist's top half exploded. Green goo splattered all over Candace.

"Oh, geez, he just candaced all over me," said an alien.

"Ewwww," said Candace.

"Oh, don't worry," Super Super Big Doctor said, waving away Candace's concern. "He'll grow back."

An alien then escorted Stapler Fist's still-walking legs toward the door.

"Wow," Candace said. "It really *does* sound like my name."

"It happens whenever they get excited," Super Super Big Doctor explained. "Especially when they get free stuff. Birthdays here are a bloodbath. Now just relax. We're gonna have a beautiful day."

* * *

While Candace enjoyed the best, most beautiful day of her life, Phineas, Ferb, and their friends trudged through a weird alien jungle.

Sorry, forgot to mention Dr. Doofenshmirtz; he was there, too. But he's not really a friend, right? More of an acquaintance.

Oh, also Agent P. He was there, too, but

following behind Phineas and Ferb so he wouldn't be seen.

"This way!" Isabella shouted. "The fortress is three klicks away."

"Wait a minute," Dr. Doofenshmirtz said, confused. "What's a click? And who put you in charge, young lady? I'm the grown-up."

"Well, some people think I'm a natural leader," Isabella replied. Then she unfurled her Fireside

Girls sash, revealing dozens upon dozens of patches. There were patches for aquatic safety and aeronautics and shrimp-net repair and sap collecting and saying a word no one else in the room knows—and that was just for starters.

Dr. Doofenshmirtz looked at the patches, then reached into his pocket and pulled out a card.

"Well, but have you got . . . one of *these*?" he said, and showed the card to Isabella.

"That's a library card, and yes, I do."

"Well, it doesn't matter, because I'm the adult!" Dr. Doofenshmirtz insisted. "So step aside! Doof is in charge!"

Dr. Doofenshmirtz looked around the jungle for a moment. He chose a direction and started to walk with authority as he glared at Isabella.

He took two steps before he fell into a pit.

"I'm okay!" Dr. Doofenshmirtz shouted from the bottom of the pit. "The water at the bottom broke my fall. Awfully hot, though."

Suddenly, Dr. Doofenshmirtz screamed as the water erupted, ejecting him from the pit. He landed on the ground with a loud thud.

"So, I've given this path a thorough checking out and can confidently say that we should go *that* way."

Chapter 12

"So, we all agree that we've passed this spot, somewhere between once and eleven times, right?" Dr. Doofenshmirtz said wearily. His head was bandaged, his clothes were torn, and he was limping.

"Yes!" everyone responded in unison.

Behind them, Agent P was keeping out of sight. Above them was the sound of flapping wings,

followed by a large dragon-like creature flying right at them. The monster screeched, fangs exposed.

"Okay, well, that is something you do not see every day," Dr. Doofenshmirtz observed.

That was when he pulled the Chicken-Replace-inator from his tattered clothing. One press of the trigger and a beam struck the dragon.

A moment later, a chicken was in its place.

"What just happened?" a shocked Phineas asked.

"Well, thanks to my handy Chicken-Replace-inator—which *some* people said I shouldn't bring—it switched places with the nearest chicken. Wherever that is," Dr. Doofenshmirtz said.

Dr. Doofenshmirtz was in midstride

when he fell into another pit—which led to a very steep hill. The scientist rolled down the hill until he slammed into a stone wall.

(Psssst! The stone wall was the alien fortress.)
"Oh, look!" Dr. Doofenshmirtz said. "We're here! See? I told ya I knew the way!"

* * *

"And now it's time for *Wakey Wakey, Feebla-Oot*, with your hosts Throat Lobster and Boooooooooooooot!"

The alien announcer's voice whipped the crowd into a frenzy, and they began to applaud as Throat Lobster and Boooooooooooooooot walked out on the stage.

"Thanks, everyone!" Throat Lobster said. "Please welcome Super Super Big Doctor and . . . the Chosen One!"

There was more applause as Candace and Super Super Big Doctor walked onstage. Smiling, Candace threw up peace signs with her fingers.

"The Chosen One is in the house!" she said.

"Isn't she just the best?" Super Super Big Doctor said.

"Yes, she is the best!" the studio audience echoed in agreement.

"So, Chosen One, how does it feel to be the most special being
in the whole
universe?" Throat
Lobster asked.

The audience
cheered until Super
Super Big Doctor
put a finger to her

lips. Then the audience quieted immediately.

"It feels great," Candace answered.

"For the first time ever, I feel like . . . someone. Like I matter."

"Awwwww," Super Super Big Doctor said,

and the audience imitated her.

"Aren't they both just incredible, folks?" Throat Lobster said.

Applause erupted from the crowd again, and Candace and Super Super Big Doctor both said, "Oh, you're too kind."

"Jinx!" they shouted together.

They shook hands, exchanging an increasingly complex series of gestures.

"That's just a thing we do," Candace said.

"And now, I believe our leader has a special treat for our special guest," Throat Lobster said.

Super Super Big Doctor turned to Candace, her face quite serious. "When I scoured the universe for Remarkalonium, I didn't know that I'd also find . . . a sister," she said.

"Awwwwww!" the audience roared.

"Candace, would you do me the honor of singing a power ballad with me?"

"Would I!" Candace said enthusiastically. She jumped to her feet as aliens appeared from the wings, handing cordless microphones to her and

Super Super Big Doctor. They walked out to the center of the stage and turned to face each other. Music began to play. Candace opened her mouth, ready to sing.

"Candace!"

Candace whipped her head around to see Phineas!

"Candace! We're here!" Phineas shouted. "Oh, we were so worried about you!"

Phineas was standing on the stage now, along with Ferb, Isabella, Baljeet, Buford (why did he have a canoe?), and some guy with a really long nose.

"What are you doing here?" Candace said.

"Who is this?" Super Super Big Doctor asked.

"These are my brothers," Candace said. Then, looking at their friends, she added, "Et cetera." Then, staring at Dr. Doofenshmirtz, she added, "No idea who that is."

"Oh, I'm Heinz!" Dr. Doofenshmirtz said. "I'm looking for my daughter, Vanessa. Wears black."

"I sent her off in an escape pod," Candace said. "She should be back on Earth by now!"

"Well, that's a relief," Dr. Doofenshmirtz replied. "She's out of danger."

Chapter 13

Vanessa had come face to face with an alien dragon, so she was anything *but* out of danger.

That's it. That's the chapter.

Sorry if you wanted more.

Chapter 14

"We saw you get abducted, Candace!"
Phineas said. "We came to rescue you!"

"Rescue me?" Candace said. "From *what*? A
planet where people worship me? A place where
I'm finally *special*? I'm the Chosen One!"

Candace gestured to the audience. They
began to chant, *"Cho-sen One! Cho-sen One!"*

"Oh, well, that's neat," Phineas said, not
knowing what else to say. "But, uh, chosen for
what, exactly?"

"To save the planet, okay?" Candace said.
"Ugh, why don't you want me to be happy?"

"We do, Candace," Phineas said. "Actually, we
made you a gift."

Candace stared at Phineas for a moment, then said, "Y'know what? I don't want it."

"But—"

"I have everything I ever wanted right here," Candace said, looking at Super Super Big Doctor. "She gets me. I finally feel like the universe isn't against me. And I think . . . that's because you guys aren't around."

Phineas and Ferb stared at Candace. Her words hit like a sledgehammer. They were hurt and speechless.

"I think perhaps you should give her a little space," Super Super Big Doctor said,

joining Candace. "Don't worry, Candy Cane. I'll take care of these guys."

"Would you?" Candace asked. "You're the best."

Super Super Big Doctor nodded toward an alien guard. "Braxington Ton, could you find a spot for our guests to relax?"

"If you'll follow me," Braxington Ton said, "I'll take you to your accommodations."

"Candace!" Phineas shouted.

As Braxington Ton took Phineas, Ferb, their friends, and that weird guy with the long nose away, Candace's eyes met her brothers'.

She was about to say something when Super Super Big Doctor hollered, "Give it up for the Chosen One!"

The audience broke out into applause and

cheers once more as Candace looked away from her brothers.

* * *

The sound of applause faded as Phineas, Ferb, and their friends were escorted down the fortress hallway by Braxington Ton.

"I can't believe Candace," Phineas said. "I mean, I know sometimes she seems kinda . . ."

"Obsessive?" Isabella offered.

"Volatile?" Baljeet suggested.

"Enchanting?" Buford swooned. "I mean, uh, terrifying?"

"I was gonna say unhappy," Phineas replied. "But I had no idea how unhappy she's been."

Braxington Ton stopped the group as they arrived at a door. Inside, the group found what looked like a very posh alien hotel room.

"Well, this is a step up from that horrifying jungle," Dr. Doofenshmirtz said. "I guess it pays to know the Chosen O—"

Before Dr. Doofenshmirtz could finish his sentence, the floor dropped out beneath him, Phineas, Ferb, Isabella, Buford, and Baljeet. They slid down a long metal chute until they landed inside a windowless room.

"Hey, where's my canoe?" Buford asked.

As if in answer, something hit the doctor on the head.

"*Ow!*" Dr. Doofenshmirtz exclaimed.

"Oh, there it is," Buford said.

"Not to sound alarmist," Baljeet said, "but did anyone else notice that they dropped us down a trapdoor into a shaft that launched us into this

truck, which is driving us who knows where?"

Oh, that's right—it wasn't a windowless room. It was a windowless *truck*.

Phineas looked around the back

of the truck and saw a group of aliens he hadn't noticed before.

"Hi there," Phineas said. "Do you fellas know where this bus goes?"

"W-we're going to prison," one of them said.

"What?" Phineas exclaimed.

"That Super Super Big Doofus sent us up the river!" Isabella said angrily.

"Well, if you hadn't insisted on leading, we probably wouldn't be in this mess," the doctor said.

"Do you see this patch?" Isabella said,

pointing to her sash. "Pray you never find out what it's for."

"Okay," Phineas said, "while I love ominous patch-related threats more than anyone—"

Ferb cut off his brother by clearing his throat.

"Right, apart from Ferb. Big fan," Phineas said.

"The bottom line is we're in trouble. And I have a feeling Candace is, too."

As the vehicle drove by on its way to the prison, something small and teal jumped from the

bushes. It landed on the alien vehicle and quickly attached itself to the underside.

Agent P was sticking close.

Chapter 15

Inside the grand dining hall, Super Super Big Doctor held court from the end of a long table. The place settings were elegant, and the spread of alien foods was a feast fit for a Chosen One. It was good fortune that they just happened to have a Chosen One present.

As Candace walked into the dining hall, aliens dropped flower petals at her feet.

"There she is!" Super Super Big Doctor called. "The Chosen One is in the dining room!"

"Oh, uh, thanks," Candace said. She sat down next to the alien as the feast began.

"Listen," Super Super Big Doctor said with a

chuckle, "I was proud of you today. You really stood up for yourself."

Candace gave her new friend a weak smile. "You don't think I was, I dunno, a little too hard on my brothers?"

"Heck no, girl!" Super Super Big Doctor said. "You don't need them coming in here, messing up things for you."

"I guess you're right," Candace said, but she wasn't so sure.

"Trust me," Super Super Big Doctor said bitterly. "Same story with my brothers. Everyone thought they were soooo special. So I had to find my own place in the universe, just like you're doing right now."

An alien came to the leader and whispered something in her ear. "I gotta go deal with some boring leader-y stuff," Super Super Big Doctor said. "You stay here, eat, drink—and don't forget to breathe. A *lot*. If you need anything, just ask."

"Oh, I do have a . . . " Candace said.

But Super Super Big Doctor had already left the dining hall. Candace sighed and slumped in her chair. Her eyes traveled to the ceiling, and she noticed a pipe that connected to a closed door.

"Hey," Candace said to an alien standing nearby, "do you know where that pipe goes?"

"Rrrrrrrrrr," the alien said, and Candace didn't understand what that meant.

"Uh, never mind. I'll figure it out myself." Candace got up from the table and left.

If she had stayed for just a few more seconds, she would have heard the alien say, "Rrrrrrruuuuunnnn!"

* * *

Inside the windowless alien vehicle, Phineas, Ferb, and their friends searched desperately for a means of escape. Isabella took a Fireside Girls multi-tool from her pocket and tried to pry loose some of the bolts on the wall. It was no use.

"Soon as we get to prison, I'm gonna start a gang," Buford said. "Who's in?"

71

"Oh, oh, me!" Baljeet said cheerfully.

"Anyone?" Buford asked again.

"Me! Me! *Me!*" Baljeet yelled.

"Anyone at all?" Buford asked.

Phineas approached the aliens. "Hi, again," he said softly. "There's no reason to be scared of us."

"Oh, we don't need a reason," the alien said. "We're afraid of a lot of things. Things like loud noises, our shadows, the dark, public speaking, cloudy skies, clear skies . . ."

Phineas could only stare silently as the alien kept talking and the list of things that scared them got longer.

* * *

Agent P climbed the side of the transport. A guard sat at a gunner station atop the vehicle. Agent P crept stealthily up the turret, his tiny arm reaching up for the guard. He yanked the alien from his perch and hurled him off.

As the body hit the ground, a soft *candace* could be heard. Agent P glanced behind him and saw a pair of alien legs walking away.

* * *

". . . and we're *also* afraid of monsters, clowns, spiders, spiders who look like clowns, cracks in the sidewalk . . ."

As Phineas, Isabella, Buford, Baljeet, and Dr. Doofenshmirtz listened to the seemingly endless list of fears, Ferb went to work on a floor panel. In no time, he removed it and began stripping away some electrical wires.

"Oh, great idea, Ferb!" Phineas said. "Maybe if we remove some of these components, it will stop the vehicle!"

* * *

Outside, Agent P clung to the vehicle, inching his way toward the drivers. Suddenly, his communicator came to life and Major Monogram's voice could be heard.

That drew the attention of the drivers.

"Oh, Agent P," Major Monogram said. "I completely forgot to tell you: whatever you do, do *not* engage in any kind of physical conflict with the aliens. It could put you in violation of numerous intergalactic treaties."

Agent P chittered.

* * *

Inside the vehicle, Phineas sat atop Dr. Doofenshmirtz's shoulders. Using the electrical wires Ferb had obtained, he was trying to short out the vehicle by fiddling with the light fixture.

Every time he connected the wires, it caused a spark. The vehicle jolted.

"It's working!" Isabella said.

* * *

Except it wasn't really working. The jolting of the vehicle came about because Agent P was busy

fighting the alien drivers. Every time Phineas connected the wires, it coincided with Agent P hitting the drivers, causing them to momentarily lose control of the vehicle.

Agent P was thrown out of the vehicle. While hanging from a door handle, he managed to fire his grappling hook, which lodged itself in the back of the driver's seat.

As they zoomed past a large tree, Agent P hooked his grappling gun to a limb. The entire driver's seat was ripped out of the vehicle, and the driver along with it.

Agent P jumped back into the cab and knocked the other driver right into a pond.

* * *

"We stopped," Isabella said.

The back doors to the vehicle opened, and Phineas, Ferb, and their friends emerged.

"Hmm, that's weird," Phineas said. "No guards, no nothing."

"Coming through!" one of the aliens said.

"The patrols will be here any minute!" another alien added. "Follow us!"

Agent P watched as the aliens hurried away with his human family, those other kids, and Dr. Doofenshmirtz in tow.

Chapter 16

Phineas, Ferb, Isabella, Buford, Baljeet, and Dr. Doofenshmirtz had trekked through the dense alien jungle with their new alien . . . Well, is "friends" the right word? In the spirit of intergalactic amity, let's call them friends.

The group had come to learn that the leader of the recently freed aliens was named Borthos.

"Finally, a place of safety," Borthos said. "Behold! The hidden city of Cowardalia!"

Then he approached a rock and pressed a hidden button. The rock split in two, parting like a curtain, and the group entered.

"An old, dark cave?" Buford asked. "You must be very proud."

"Oh, no, this is just the entrance," Borthos said.

Borthos showed them what looked like some kind of boat, and they hopped in. The alien guided the boat down a river inside the cave, sailing past statues of other aliens, who appeared to be cowering in fear.

"Behold! The city of Cowardalia!" Borthos repeated.

"You live in these big statues?" Buford asked.

"Oh, uh, no. No, those are just monuments we built up," Borthos said, clearly exasperated. "The city is beyond those."

The ship sailed past the statues until it arrived at an opening, revealing a cavern filled with huts.

"Behold! The hidden city of Cowardalia!"

"Really, Ernox?" Borthos said, staring at the alien who had just upstaged him. *"Really?"*

"Borthos!" shouted Garnoz, another alien. "You escaped from the Scary Ones! Did you hide under a tarp? Did you cower under some  boxes? Did you stand very still and pretend to be modern art?"

"No," Borthos said. "These aliens helped us escape." Borthos pointed toward Phineas.

"Thank you for saving my people," Garnoz said. "You may hide and cower with us here in Cowardalia for as long as you wish."

"Thanks," Phineas said. "But we're worried about our sister. We've gotta get back to her!"

"And I have to get back to my daughter on Earth," Dr. Doofenshmirtz added.

"We would love to help you," Garnoz said. "But we can't.

"Let me explain," Garnoz continued. "We used to be a free and happy cowardly people. Then one day, *she* arrived.

"And she brought her evil plant of doom," Garnoz continued. "She sprayed us with mind-controlling spores. She forced us to build her

castles, lavish her with treasures, and make low-quality TV shows. Then, one day, the spores began to disappear. Our minds became clear, so we did the only thing that we could do. We ran away like frightened toddlers.

"Sadly, some of our people are still under her control. And now we hear that she has found someone with the power to make her sinister shrubbery grow once more."

Phineas and Ferb exchanged looks. Then the entire group said, "The Chosen One!"

Phineas looked out at his friends and the assembled aliens. "Listen, everyone," he began. "We came all the way across the

universe to save our sister. And we're not going home without her. If you care about your people as much as we care about Candace, then, please, help us!"

"You do not understand," Garnoz protested. "All we do is cower. We are called the Cowards. In our language, it means 'coward.'"

"Just because you *are* Cowards doesn't mean you have to *be* cowards," Phineas said. "And if you can be brave just this once, from here on, 'Coward' could mean 'mighty warrior'!"

* * *

Candace was walking down a corridor, glancing up at the pipe that followed the ceiling. It led to an imposing set of doors. When she stood before them, the doors opened. Candace saw a plant inside. Next to it was a sign that said YOU MUST BE AT LEAST THIS TALL TO PRODUCE MIND-CONTROLLING SPORES!

Candace leaned in close, breathing on the plant.

Suddenly, it grew—just a bit, but enough to be noticed. Candace jumped back.

Turning around, Candace saw Super Super Big Doctor along with several guards.

"I see you've met Mama!" Super Super Big Doctor said.

"This plant is your mother?"

"No, silly," Super Super Big Doctor replied. "I named her after my mother . . . whose name just happened to be

Mama. She was also green and very controlling."

"What's it for?" Candace asked, looking at the suspiciously huge plant.

"It's for you!" Super Super Big Doctor said. "Check this out. Bring in the device!"

A part of the floor shifted as what looked like a treadmill rose, and Super Super Big Doctor gently led Candace over to it. "Remarkalonium is Mama's lifeblood," she said. "She'll shrivel up and die without it. Hop up here."

The alien motioned for Candace to get on the treadmill, which she did. The treadmill started to roll, and Candace began to keep pace with it.

"Thanks to you, now she can grow again and produce her wonderful mind-controlling spores!"

"Oh, so I'm actually doing something— *waaaait*," Candace said. "Mind-controlling *spores*?"

"How do you think I got to be in charge in the

first place?" Super Super Big Doctor said. "But now the spores have been wearing off. See?"

Super Super Big Doctor pointed at one of the Cowards, who looked like his head was

slowly clearing. The alien then dropped the tray he was carrying and ran right out the door.

When no one did anything, Super Super Big Doctor turned to look at her minions. "Really?" she said.

"What you're doing is . . . is awful!" Candace said. "How would your brothers feel if they could see you now?"

"Why don't you ask 'em?" Super Super Big Doctor suggested.

Behind her, a screen came to life, broadcasting an image of Super Super Big Doctor's siblings. They were inside

a cage, wearing tattered clothes and throwing a makeshift ball around.

"Hey!" Super Super Big Doctor shouted. "I told you no playing in the dungeon!" She pushed a button, and a ray dissolved the ball into nothingness.

"How could you imprison your own brothers?" Candace asked, horrified.

"Oh, it was easy," Super Super Big Doctor said. "I lured 'em in with these cheesy snacks—"

"No, I mean, how *could* you? I'd never do something like that to my brothers!"

"You already did," Super Super Big

Doctor said. "I said, 'I'll take care of 'em,' and *you* were like, 'Would you? You're the best.'

So I thought you were down with the whole dungeon thing!"

Candace was fuming. "Wait, you threw my brothers in the dungeon? That's not what I wanted! I *love* my brothers!"

"Wow," Super Super Big Doctor said. "Wow. Candy, Candy, Candy. This is eye-opening. Have I misread things or what?"

"Yeah, I'd say you have. So can we—"

Suddenly, Super Super Big Doctor pressed a button, and handcuffs snapped around Candace's wrists, confining her to the treadmill.

"Hey! Let me go!"

"I guess it was too good to be true," Super Super Big Doctor said, shaking her head.

"I thought I finally found someone simpatico. And you even exhaled Remarkalonium."

"Remarkalonium," Candace scoffed. "What *is* that, anyway? Is that even *real*?"

"Of course! In your language, I think it's called . . . carbon dioxide or CO_2."

"Wait, your 'rare element' is carbon dioxide?" Candace snorted. "*Everybody* exhales carbon dioxide!"

"Uh, no we don't," Super Super Big Doctor said. "We inhale oxygen *and* exhale oxygen."

"Well, on Earth, *everybody* exhales carbon dioxide, genius," Candace said snarkily.

Suddenly, a strange look came over the alien leader's face. "Hold up, hold up, hold up. What?"

"Yeah! All seven billion of us!" Candace said, taunting her. "You didn't even realize I'm not . . . I'm not . . . special," Candace finished, realizing the same thing herself.

Super Super Big Doctor grinned. "If all you Earthlings exhale carbon dioxide, I can feed Mama *forever*! And I can have hundreds of castles and smoothies and TV shows! Braxington Ton! Fire up the ship! We have an even *bigger* planet to conquer!"

"Wait, *no*!" Candace shouted.

Chapter 17

"Load up the portable CO_2 generator," Super Super Big Doctor said, pointing at Candace. She smirked at her newest prisoner. "Been a heck of a day for you, huh? Threw your brothers in jail, then threw your whole planet under the bus. Heh . . . nice going . . . *sister*."

A guard approached the treadmill with a remote and moved Candace out the door. "All right, this way, Chosen One," the guard said.

Leaving the fortress, Candace could see Super Super Big Doctor ahead. She was taking the giant plant, Mama, with her to Earth.

"Now make sure Mama is comfortable," Super Super Big Doctor ordered.

Before she could give another order, something distracted the leader. Candace heard it, too.

"Wait! What am I hearing right now?" Super Super Big Doctor asked.

"I think it's music, ma'am," a guard replied.

Looking over the edge of the launchpad, the leader saw Phineas and Ferb, along with an army of aliens. Somehow, they had escaped. And they appeared to be armed, too.

But before this gathering army was going to

do anything, they were apparently going to sing a song about fighting or something. Not only that, the song revealed that the army was going to *appear* to attack on the left, but in reality, the bulk of their forces was going to attack on the right.

"The fools!" Super Super Big Doctor spat.

"They're telling us their entire plan—in song! Get our forces over to the right!"

"Yeah, okay, boss," said one of the guards. "Uh . . . their right, or *our* right?"

"No, *our* right!" the kids and the Cowards sang out.

* * *

Super Super Big Doctor stood near the wall on the right with dozens upon dozens of guards. "As soon as they scale the wall, let 'em have it!" she ordered.

But when she looked over the wall, no one was there.

"What?" the leader said, bewildered.

"Psych!" Buford shouted. "We're over here."

Had Super Super Big Doctor been drinking a cup of coffee, she would have spat it all over. To her surprise and chagrin, she was now surrounded by Phineas, Ferb, their friends, and the Cowards.

"We came in on the left while you were going over to the right," Buford explained.

"You lied to us!" Super Super Big Doctor fumed. "Through song—an art form that's supposed to connect people through sincerity of emotion! That is cold. Who *are* you people?"

"We are the Cowards!" Borthos shouted.

"Well, I'm a big enough woman to admit when—*Run!*" Super Super Big Doctor screamed.

At once, the leader and her guards scattered.

"Let's go find Candace!" Phineas said.

Before they even took a step, Ferb pointed at a landing pad in the distance. The mother ship was there, and they could see Candace on a treadmill, being pushed toward it.

"Candace!" Phineas shouted, but his sister was too far away to hear him.

* * *

"Activate anti-Coward countermeasures!" Super Super Big Doctor ordered as she ran up the ramp to the mother ship.

The Cowards followed but stopped in their tracks when a spider decoy popped up before them. The "spider" made a scary sound—or at least, it was scary to the Cowards.

* * *

Meanwhile, Phineas, Ferb, and their friends were racing toward the launchpad. Along the way, Dr. Doofenshmirtz's phone pinged.

"It's Vanessa!
She's *not* back on
Earth! She's still on
this planet!"

He showed
everyone a selfie
Vanessa had taken.

"I'll save Vanessa," Dr. Doofenshmirtz said.
"You guys go, while you still can!"

"How'll you get back to Earth?" Isabella asked.

"By adulting!" the doctor said, locking eyes with
Isabella. "I learned from the best. Go! Go now!"

Isabella looked at the doctor with approval,
then slapped a patch on his sleeve.

"What's this?" Dr. Doofenshmirtz asked.

"It's a 'getting back to Earth' patch," Isabella
said. "Earn it!"

93

Behind them, Agent P stuck out his head, watching the kids and then Dr. Doofenshmirtz. He had an impossible choice: follow his enemy or his family? Either way, they both needed saving.

* * *

"Borthos, no!" Garnoz screamed. "You'll be killed!"

Spear in hand, Borthos was closing in on the painted spider thingy.

Before he could do anything, Phineas, Ferb, Isabella, Buford, and Baljeet ran right past him and smashed through the spider.

"Oh, they're so brave!" one of the Cowards shouted.

Phineas, Ferb, and their friends managed to climb onto the ramp and get inside.

Then the mother ship blasted off.

For Earth.

Chapter 18

"All right," Dr. Doofenshmirtz said, fiddling with his phone. "Maybe I can figure out where Vanessa is from this photo."

He tilted the phone, looking at the picture, then comparing it with the fortress.

"There we go! So she must be that way!"

Looking over the wall, he saw the jungle before him and took a deep breath, followed by a few steps, followed by a tumble over the edge.

But before he could hit the ground, Agent P appeared. He dove after Doof and caught him. Agent P shot out his hand, grabbing a branch and preventing both from falling to their doom.

"Perry the Platypus!" Dr. Doofenshmirtz said.

"Have you been following me? All the way from Earth? Keeping me safe and protecting me from like a fuzzy teal guardian angel?"

Agent P looked at the doctor and then shrugged as if to say, *Sure.*

Crack!

The branch snapped, and they both fell.

Before they could reach the ground, a flying dragon creature swooped in, snatching them both. Dr. Doofenshmirtz was shocked to see that Vanessa was riding the dragon.

"Vanessa?" shouted Dr. Doofenshmirtz.

"I thought it was you guys!" Vanessa said. "How did you get here?"

"Oh, I—I have no idea how Perry the Platypus got here," the doctor said. "But I used my Galactic Travel-inator."

"You mean your spaceship?"

"Hey, where did you get the alien dragon creature?" the doctor asked.

"You like her?" Vanessa asked, patting the dragon. "I named her Vlorkel. Can I keep her?"

"Well," Dr. Doofenshmirtz said, "we're gonna need a bigger litter box."

* * *

Phineas, Ferb, Isabella, Buford, and Baljeet were stowaways aboard the alien mother ship.

"We need to find where they're keeping Candace," Phineas said.

"Hey, look!" Buford said, pointing to a monitor. "They're takin' us back to Earth!"

"More likely they wanna conquer Earth!" Phineas said, correcting him.

"Attention," said a computer voice. "Brace yourselves. We are accelerating to warp two."

"Oh, my, that is twice the speed of light!" Baljeet exclaimed.

* * *

Vlorkel landed in a clearing, and Vanessa, her dad, and Agent P climbed off. Dr. Doofenshmirtz hugged his daughter tightly.

"Oh, Dad," Vanessa said, "I can't believe you came to save me."

"And then you saved me!" Dr. Doofenshmirtz said. "But I don't know how we're gonna get home from here."

Suddenly, they heard the cluck of a chicken.

"That's it!" Dr. Doofenshmirtz exclaimed. "We'll use the Chicken-Replace-inator to switch places with a chicken on Earth! It worked like a charm earlier. Come on! Get on!"

Dr. Doofenshmirtz climbed back onto Vlorkel, helping Vanessa on as well. Then Agent P hopped on. The doctor aimed the Chicken-Replace-inator at them like he was taking a selfie with his phone. When he pressed the trigger, there was a brilliant flash of light.

Where once sat a Vlorkel, there was now a chicken.

The chicken that had been sitting just a few feet away.

"Wait a second," Dr. Doofenshmirtz said.

Chapter 19

"We've gotta find a way to stop this ship," Phineas said.

"Oooh! *Space Adventure*," Baljeet offered. "In episode 347A! Captain Dirk Mortenson and the lovely Lieutenant Zarna, who was secretly—"

"Baljeet!" Phineas, Ferb, Isabella, and Buford screamed.

"Sorry. We can use the shield generator to overload the main reactor and disable the ship, stranding them in orbit," Baljeet said.

The kids raced to a control panel and looked at the assortment of lights, switches, and buttons.

"Are you sure you know what you're doing?" Phineas asked.

"In *Space Adventure*, it is always the leftmost button," Baljeet replied.

Before anyone could stop him, Baljeet pressed a button on the control panel. The shuttle bay doors opened, sucking everything out into the upper atmosphere . . . including the kids!

They were now falling through the air, junk from the shuttle bay all around them, as the mother ship rocketed toward Earth.

"We are never listening to another *Space Adventure* idea!" Buford yelled.

"I don't have a patch for surviving a fall because of the false science of a canceled TV show!" Isabella lamented.

"Hey, I got an idea!" Buford said. "Everybody into the canoe!"

Everyone clambered into the canoe.

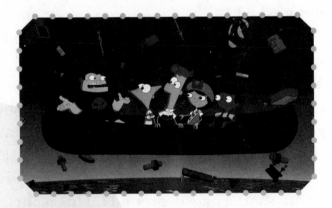

"What do we do now?" Phineas asked.

"I don't know," Buford said. "I didn't think that far ahead."

"Hey, we can use this debris just like they did in *Space Adventure* episode 436B!" Phineas said.

"All right, let's do it!" Buford said.

"Oh, yeah!" Isabella seconded.

"Wait, *Space Adventure*? Why is it a good idea when Phineas says it?" Baljeet asked.

"Everybody, grab something!" Phineas said. The kids started to grab all kinds of space junk as they plummeted toward the ground.

Buford looked up to see exactly what they had been building. It looked kind of like a boat, except this boat was built in the canoe.

"You made another boat?" Buford said. "What have I been luggin' this one around for?"

Ferb pulled a cord. In a flash, the "boat" transformed into a glider.

Except they were still heading straight for the ground.

103

"Pull up, pull up, pull up!" Buford shouted.

At the last possible moment, right before impact, the glider pulled out of its dive.

Buford patted the canoe and looked at Isabella. "And you said we wouldn't need it."

"Look, gang, there's our house!" Phineas said, pointing below. "Put her down there, Ferb! We got some building to do!"

Chapter 20

The mother ship had descended on Danville Stadium, home of the Narwhals baseball team. The mayor was on hand to unveil a new statue of the founder of the Tri-State Area, John P. Tri-State. The unveiling went according to plan, if you consider having a gigantic alien mother ship

crush the statue along with a decent chunk of a baseball stadium going according to plan.

"Hey!" said some random man. "Is that an alien spaceship?"

The crowd murmured, "Yes, yes it is."

A ramp extended from the mother ship, and Super Super Big Doctor disembarked, flanked by her guards. Mama was in tow as the guards fanned out, carrying blasters.

"People of Earth!" Super Super Big Doctor exclaimed. "Breathe on me! Or, more to the point, breathe on my plant of doom!"

Mama seemed to be getting bigger every second, absorbing carbon dioxide from Earth's natural atmosphere.

"Not so fast!" Phineas shouted from atop the scoreboard. "No, really. Don't breathe so fast. It makes the plant grow! And trust me, that's bad."

"What in the . . ." Super Super Big Doctor said, astounded.

The kids each pulled out a remote control unit. They pressed the buttons, and a rumble filled the air as giant rolling robots thundered into the stadium.

"Oh, no!" Super Super Big Doctor said, feigning fear. "What are we gonna—*Thermal cannon!*"

The alien leader's order was carried out immediately as the thermal cannon fired, reducing the kids' giant robots to ashes in a second.

Then the thermal cannon was trained on the kids.

"Uh, guys?" Isabella said, pointing this out. The kids dove from the scoreboard onto the playing field just as the thermal cannon blasted

the scoreboard into itty-bitty scoreboard pieces.

The crowds of people in the bleachers fled.

"Soak up that carbon dioxide, Mama!" Super Super Big Doctor said.

As the crowd ran from the stadium, an oblivious

Jeremy stayed at his post in the Slushy Dog truck. Busy preparing his live-action role-playing gear, he wasn't aware of anything outside—until

someone dove into the truck to escape
the madness.

"Wow, Jeremy," Stacy said. "You're already
getting ready to fend off the alien invasion!"

"There's an alien invasion?" Jeremy asked. He
turned from his LARP equipment and saw the
hordes of people running and screaming.

* * *

"Ferb and I have gotta get on that ship and get
to Candace," Phineas said.

"Go for it!" Isabella said. "We'll run interference!"

"Yeah, I'm great at interfering!" Buford insisted, and he was not incorrect.

Buford disappeared from the dugout, followed by Isabella and Baljeet.

A moment later, the doors to the clubhouse opened, and the Narwhals' golf cart careened

onto the playing field. Buford was behind the wheel, thoroughly enthused. Baljeet sat beside him, holding a rake, while Isabella threw chalk bombs at the aliens.

"Eat canoe, alien freak boys!" Buford shouted. His precious canoe was tied to the back of the golf cart, knocking over alien guards as they drove. "We're using it again!" he pointed out, nodding toward the canoe.

"Yeah, yeah, I'll make you a patch," Isabella said, shaking her head.

Chapter 21

Candace was on the bridge of the mother ship, slumped over on the treadmill. She was stumbling over her feet as the treadmill slowly cranked on. Monitors surrounded her, and the chaos from the baseball stadium filled the screens. But Candace didn't even look up.

An alien guard, who presumably was supposed to be watching Candace, was on the phone instead.

"Hey, Sand Toaster!" the alien said. "You're never gonna guess where I am. Her Highness put me in charge of the Chosen One!"

The alien on the other end of the line babbled excitedly.

"Ha ha, that's right! She's on a treadmill, making a lot of CO_2, and let me tell you, this is the big time. Ol' Toilet Flower here is going places!"

The alien on the other end of the line babbled even more excitedly than the first time.

"You're under attack?" Toilet Flower said. "Oh, wow, from who? Let me go to the monitors."

Toilet Flower looked at the monitors and saw utter chaos outside. "Oh, yeah, I see ya there," he said. "Oh, wow, you *are* under attack."

Candace, her eyes heavy, her feet tired and sore, looked up at the monitors. She was absolutely floored to see, among all the activity, Phineas and Ferb sneaking up the ramp of the mother ship.

"They . . . they escaped?" Candace said quietly. "But how did they make it back to Earth?"

"Let me see what else is going on," Toilet Flower said to the alien on the phone. "I think I'll check this monitor to my left."

"Uh, hey, excuse me, Mr. Toilet Shower?" Candace said, trying to get his attention.

"Toilet *Flower*," the alien insisted.

"Oh, sorry. Hey, these shoes pinch. Yeah, I'd be able to create much more carbon dioxide if you just loosened them a teensy bit."

But Toilet Shower—sorry, *Flower*—wasn't paying attention. He was still on the phone. At least he wasn't looking at the monitor, so he wouldn't see Phineas and Ferb sneaking aboard.

"I gotta let you go," Toilet Flower said, then hung up the phone. "All right," he said to Candace. "I want you makin' a lot of CO_2."

He loosened Candace's shoes and turned his head slightly—almost, but not quite, enough to see Phineas and Ferb on the monitor.

Thinking fast, Candace kicked Toilet Flower

in the chest. He fell right over onto the treadmill. Then she stomped on him.

Toilet Flower screamed, "It's the worst pain I've ever felt! I can't believe you did this to me!"

Then Candace kicked the remote on Toilet Flower's belt into her hands as he was practically consumed by the treadmill.

"It's so much worse underneath!" Toilet Flower yelled.

Pressing a button, Candace released the handcuffs.

The treadmill spat out Toilet Flower, and he landed in a ball right in front of Phineas and Ferb as they entered.

"Candace!" Phineas shouted.

"Phineas and Ferb!" Candace said. Then she ran toward a nearby alcove, sobbing.

"Candace, are you okay?" Phineas asked.

"I'm just so ashamed," Candace said with a sniffle. "I can't believe you guys came to save me after all those awful things I said. After everything I've done, all summer . . . I've been ruining everyone's fun."

"What are you talking about?" Phineas asked.

"I'm not the Chosen One. I'm not special. I'm not even a good sister," Candace said mournfully. "You guys are better off without me."

"Candace, open our gift," Phineas said.

"The gift?" Candace said. "Oh, you were even trying to give me a gift, and I wouldn't take it. I'm so horrible!"

"Please, Candace," Phineas said, handing the present to his sister. "Open it."

Candace did. It was a mug that said WORLD'S #1 SISTER.

"You got me a coffee mug," Candace said.
"And I don't even drink coffee! I can't do
anything right!"

"Push the button, Candace," Phineas said.
Only then did Candace notice a little button
on the handle. When she pressed it, the room lit
up, projecting holograms of Candace everywhere.
Each hologram showed Candace doing

something amazing: performing one-handed push-ups; wrestling an alligator; playing the bassoon, the banjo, and the bongos, all while singing.

"Wow," Candace said with a gasp. "What *is* this?"

"It's all the things that make you the coolest person we've ever met," Phineas said. "You kick butt! You rock out! And you can always make us laugh. The kinda laughter where stuff squirts

out of your nose.
Summer would
be no fun without
you! We just wish
you could see
yourself the way
we see you. You

may not be the Chosen One . . ."

"But we'd choose you as a sister every time,"
Ferb said, finishing his brother's sentence.

Candace looked at the holograms and then at
her brothers with tears in her eyes. "Oh, guys,"
she said.

They smiled at their sister, and for a moment,
it was possible to forget they were on an alien
mother ship.

"I could not have chosen better little brothers,"
Candace said. "And you know what? I know
what we're gonna do today. Save the world."

"That's what I'm talkin' about!" Phineas said.

"Okay. We've got to figure out a way to stop
Super Super Big Doc," Candace said. "Wait. Is
today free T-shirt day?"

"Focus, Candace," Phineas said.

"Oh, I *am*."

Chapter 22

Super Super Big Doctor smiled. Soon this foolish resistance would all be over, and she would have an endless supply of carbon dioxide and mind-controlled servants.

"Hey, Shoe Monkey!" Candace cried to one of the alien guards. "How about a free T-shirt?"

"Free stuff?" Shoe Monkey screamed. "Just like my birthday!" Instantly, Shoe Monkey became so excited that the alien's top half exploded.

All heads in the stadium whipped around to see Candace standing on the ramp of the mother ship, holding a T-shirt cannon in her arms. Normally the cannon would be used to blast T-shirts into

the crowd for cheer-happy fans. But not today. Today it would become a weapon of freedom.

"She escaped?" Super Super Big Doctor shouted. "Get them!"

"You know, I used to think the universe was against me," Candace said. "But now I realize it's *me* against the universe!"

"Us," Phineas added gently.

121

"It's us against the universe!" Candace said, amending her previous statement. "Duck!"

Then she started blasting free T-shirts at the aliens.

Throughout the stadium, the sound of *CANDACE, CANDACE, CANDACE* echoed every time an alien's top half went kablooey.

"And *you* get a shirt!" Candace shouted, blasting shirts everywhere. "And *you* get a shirt! And *you* get a shirt!"

The aliens were no match for the sheer glee of Candace's T-shirt ploy.

All save one.

Super Super Big Doctor was laughing, grinning. Menacingly.

Mama the plant had finally grown to mind-control proportions.

"Candace, what about her?" Phineas said.

Candace swung her T-shirt cannon around and leveled it at Super Super Big Doctor. But

when she tried to fire, nothing happened. "Oh, no," Candace said. "I'm all out of T-shirts!"

Suddenly, the plant began to spin, spitting mind-control spores into the stadium crowd. Almost immediately, the assembled people went into a trance. They were now under the control of Super Super Big Doctor.

"Gas masks, quick!" Phineas shouted, and the kids pulled them on.

"Ha!" Super Super Big Doctor chortled. "It's working!"

Then, to test her newfound control over the humans, she said, "Sit down!"

And the crowd sat down.

"Stand up!"

And the crowd stood up.

"Get those kids!" she screamed.

"Get those kids!" the crowd roared, and swarmed after them. The kids were outnumbered ten thousand to one.

"Run!" Phineas hollered.

But the crowd was moving too fast. They grabbed Baljeet, Buford, and Isabella and passed the kids over their heads.

"My personal space!" Baljeet screamed.

Candace looked around but didn't see any sign of her brothers. "Phineas? Ferb?" she called.

"Yoo-hoo! Over here!"

Candace turned her head to see Super Super Big Doctor aiming a blaster right at Phineas and Ferb.

"You and I need to have a little talk," the alien leader said. Super Super Big Doctor kept moving the blaster from one brother to the other and back. "I'm disappointed in you, Candy Corn."

Candace walked through the zombified crowd toward her foe.

"We coulda been something," Super Super Big Doctor said. "Two girls against the universe . . . and you threw it away. Oh, sister. You could have been special."

"I'm not your sister," Candace said, her voice strong. "And I *am* special. My brothers showed me that."

Both Phineas and Ferb *awww*ed.

"Pffft," Super Super Big Doctor said. "Brothers."

"And you know what? Maybe you should reconsider your relationship with your brothers, too," Candace said.

The alien laughed. "Why would I do that?"

"Think about it," Candace said, walking closer. "Is it possible, just possible, that this obsession you have with controlling—controlling the planet, controlling your brothers—is really just a distraction from your real problem . . . which is how you feel about yourself?"

"You mean like a . . . tiny, meaningless speck in the universe?" Super Super Big Doctor said.

"That's good, keep going. . . ."

"It's just that everyone always thought my brothers were so special," the alien said. "No one paid attention to me at all. So I made myself

special by controlling everybody else. Wait a minute. . . . This hasn't been about my brothers at all. It's just been about my own self-worth! Wow. . . . what a breakthrough!"

Candace was very nearly overjoyed that her plan had worked. We say "very nearly" because  that was when she noticed Mama growing even bigger behind Super Super Big Doctor.

"I don't need any of this!" the alien continued, not noticing the enormous plant. *"Listen!* Listen to me!"

"Yes?" the crowd replied in one voice.

"You do not have to listen to me!"

"I'm confused," everyone in the crowd said at the same time.

"I am *not* going to control you anymore! I was seeking validation through the mindless obedience of others, but no more! Because I am enough! I am spe—"

Super Super Big Doctor's big moment was thoroughly derailed when Mama gobbled her up.

Then the giant plant broke free of its base and sprouted enormous legs. It stomped through the stadium, swiping the mind-controlled minions aside with its tendrils.

"Well, that victory was short-lived," Isabella said.

Chapter 23

Things were not looking good.

"Run!" Buford shouted. "It's gaining on us!"

Suddenly, a screech came from the sky. The kids looked up, stunned to see a dragon-like creature swooping in from above. On its back were Vanessa and Dr. Doofenshmirtz.

"Quick, get on!" Vanessa said.

Vlorkel snatched up all the kids right as Mama was about to crush them.

* * *

Mama chased Vlorkel through the stadium and out into downtown Danville. Vlorkel went around buildings, under the freeway— anywhere to try to evade the enormous plant.

While the chase continued, Candace turned to Vanessa. "Wait. How did you get back to Earth?"

"The good ol' Chicken-Replace-inator," Vanessa said.

"Chicken-Replace-inator?" Candace asked.

"You shoot something; it switches places with the nearest chicken," Isabella explained.

"Vanessa remembered it had a setting for the furthest chicken," Dr. Doofenshmirtz said. "So we switched places with the furthest chicken, which was here on Earth."

Candace nodded, pretending it all made perfect sense.

Suddenly, Mama reared up in front of them.

Vlorkel recoiled and screeched. Vanessa pulled hard on the reins, causing Vlorkel to turn sharply away from Mama toward a towering radio tower. The space dragon flew upward inside the structure as Mama attempted to push the tower over onto the city below.

* * *

Agent P clung to Vlorkel's underbelly for dear

131

life. As she flew up, the tower got narrower.

* * *

Right as Vlorkel was about to free herself from the tower, Mama succeeded in pushing it over. When the kids went flying, Vlorkel scooped them up in her enormous wings.

* * *

Agent P let go of the dragon and landed on the

steel bars of the radio tower moments before it began to fall.

Downtown Danville would be crushed.

And Agent P would be crushed along with downtown Danville.

With a High-Tech Secret Agent Gadget in each furry teal webbed foot, Agent P shot out two grappling hooks. One latched on to a billboard.

The other wound around a rooftop water tank. Agent P anchored the High-Tech Secret Agent Gadgets to the tower bars.

The tower kept falling faster, faster, faster. Then a little slower. Then a lot slower. Then it stopped, twenty-six feet or so above the street.

Agent P had stopped the tower from falling!

A moment later, the tower fell right on top of Jeremy's food truck.

Candace climbed out of the tower and saw her friends. "Stacy! Jeremy!" she exclaimed.

Dr. Doofenshmirtz fell out of the tower next. Candace helped him to his feet and picked up the -inator that fell out of his pocket.

"Here you go," she said. "Wait, is this the Chicken-Replace-inator?"

"That's how we got back," the doctor said. "We switched places with a chicken on Earth."

"You mean there's a chicken on that planet?"

"Yeah, I guess," Dr. Doofenshmirtz said.

The other kids climbed free of the tower wreckage, but Vlorkel was still trapped inside.

"Cover me!" Candace said. "Something's about to switch places with a chicken."

Mama suddenly appeared, stomping toward Candace. Candace fired the Chicken-Replace-

inator, and a second later, the giant plant vanished from the face of the Earth. In its place stood . . . a chicken.

But before Candace could relax, she heard a monstrous roar. Turning her head, she saw that Mama was now behind them, inside a petting zoo! She was there with bunnies, and ponies, and even more chickens.

"Why is there a petting zoo downtown?" Candace said, freaking out.

"Yay, my petition worked!" Baljeet whooped.

"Yeah, you gotta set it for the furthest chicken," Dr. Doofenshmirtz advised her.

Mama drew closer, opening its plant jaws, threatening to devour Candace. Candace turned

the Chicken-Replace-inator's setting from NEAREST, past BEVERLY HILLS, beyond BEVERLY HILLS ADJACENT, to FURTHEST.

Right as the monstrosity tried to take a bite,
Candace fired the -inator. Mama was instantly
replaced with
another chicken.

Candace looked
around. There was
no sign of Mama
anywhere.

"Hey, look! It
worked!" Candace
said. "The spores are gone!"

Sure enough, the humans around them were
no longer under any kind of mind control. The
kids took off their gas masks.

And Agent P heaved a sigh of relief as he
snuck into the shadows.

Chapter 24

To say that downtown Danville was a complete disaster area is putting it mildly. The baseball stadium had been smashed to bits, and food trucks and cars had crashed everywhere following Mama's destructive rampage. There were crowds of people all over, wondering how they had gotten wherever it was they were.

In the thick of it all were the kids.

"Yay, you did it!" Phineas shouted to his sister.

"Yes, yes, yes, something switched places with a chicken," Candace said.

Honk!

"Candace, look! It's your mom!" Stacy said.

"If your mom sees it, she'll know you've been telling the truth—about everything!"

Candace grinned and ran toward the car.

"Moooooooooom!" she shouted.

The car screeched to a stop.

"Candace, what are you doing downtown?" her mom asked.

In that moment, Candace realized that her mom had stopped short of seeing the chaos

caused by the aliens. If she drove ahead even a little further, she would turn the corner and see everything.

"It's Phineas and Ferb," Candace said.

"What did they do now?" Mom asked, rolling her eyes.

Grinning, Candace looked back at her brothers. "They really want pizza for dinner. But from Giametti's, on the other side of town. So go that way. You gotta turn around!"

"Okay," Mom said, puzzled.

"Where's Mom going?" Phineas asked.

"She's getting us pizza," Candace replied.

"Sweet," Phineas said.

Screech!

Mom hit the brakes and leaned out the car window.

"What are you kids up to?"

"Ahh, just the usual," Candace said as she put

her arms around Phineas and Ferb. "Us against the universe."

"Okay," Mom said. "See you at home."

At last, Mom drove off.

Candace smiled at her brothers as they walked through the ruins of downtown Danville.

"You know, this morning I thought you guys were the bane of my existence," she said. "It's amazing how an afternoon of blasting aliens can really change your perspective."

As they walked along, the kids had a strange feeling that they were being followed.

Looking around, they saw a familiar web-footed, orange-beaked friend approaching.

"Oh, there you are, Perry," Phineas said.

The end!

Epilogue

Meanwhile, on Feebla-Oot, things were not so good if your name rhymed with "Super Super Big Doctor."

Or, you know, if it *was* Super Super Big Doctor.

Mama had suddenly appeared on the planet and, in one big, gross motion, hawked up the alien leader from its inside. Then the giant plant shrank and shriveled until it was only the size of a tiny sapling.

"Ohhh, Mama!" Super Super Big Doctor cried. "At least you're not completely destroyed!"

Wham!

From above, a space elephant fell, smashing what was left of Mama.

"Never mind."